Rhymin' Simon
and the
Mystery of the Fat Cat

by Bill Apablasa

and Lisa Thiesing

DUTTON CHILDREN'S BOOKS

NEW YORK

For Terri

B.A.

With thanks to Paul, the cats and our dog,

Max, for all their help and inspiration

L.T.

Speedsters is a trademark of Dutton Children's Books.

Library of Congress Cataloging-in-Publication Data

Apablasa, Bill.
  Rhymin' Simon and the mystery of the fat cat / by Bill Apablasa
and Lisa Thiesing.—1st ed.
      p.   cm.
  Summary: Rhymin' Simon, a detective who loves to make rhymes,
helps out when his neighbor's cat disappears.
    ISBN 0-525-44702-4
    [1. Cats.—Fiction.   2. Mystery and detective stories.]
I. Thiesing, Lisa.   II. Title.   90-21054
PZ7.A636Rh   1991   CIP
[Fic]—dc20   AC

Published in the United States by
Dutton Children's Books,
a division of Penguin Books USA Inc.

Printed in U.S.A.   First Edition
10 9 8 7 6 5 4 3 2 1

Chapter 1

My name is Simon, but everyone calls me Rhymin' Simon. The only thing I like better than making rhymes is solving crimes.

I'm not only the poet of my street,
but also its detective ace. So I was not
surprised when my pal, Al, came to my
place asking for help on a very strange
case.

Al's cat was lost, and Al wanted him back
at any cost.

It was a hot day, but we ran all the way to Al's house. We stopped to run through Mrs. Fisher's sprinkler. If you are a detective like me, the only rule is to stay cool.

5

When we got to Al's house, we found his sister, Annie, crying.

I patted her on the head and said, "Don't be glum, chum. I'll find that cat if it's the last thing I do. But first, tell me about him."

"Well, we haven't had Wendall all that long," said Annie.

"But he's the best and the smartest and the handsomest cat in the whole world! He lives under our porch, and I bring him food."

Yeah. Tons of food! He's also the fattest cat in the world!

Annie agreed that he *had* been getting a little heavy lately.

"Lately!?" said Al. "Every day he's getting bigger and bigger and bigger. I expect soon he's just going to explode!"

"Hmmm," I said. "Maybe your cat isn't lost. Maybe he's just out for a bite to eat."

9

"We were playing house. Wendall was my baby. He looked so cute in his blue bonnet."

"I went in to get Wendall some more milk and when I got back, he was gone."

We searched everywhere for Wendall.
We looked under bushes

and up in trees.

And, by mistake, quite near some bees.

We looked up, down and all around, but there was nothing to be found. Not even a clue. It looked hopeless.

There was only one thing left to do!

Chapter 2

I did what any good detective would do.

"And,"
I added,
"try to
get lucky
if you can."

And just as I had hoped, we got lucky.

Walking down the street came
Billy Hatcher. On any other day,
this would not
be lucky.
He was a pest.

Hi, you guys!

But today he had good news. He had
seen Al and Annie's fat cat not so long ago.

19

"Not yet, Chet. Where was he?" I asked.
First Billy pointed to the right.

Then Billy pointed to the left.

Al's and Annie's faces
turned sour.

"But," said Billy,
"I do remember
that your fat cat
was all wet. And
he had something
on his head."

"A lot of help that is," said Al.

"There's only one way a fat cat gets wet around here. I'll bet he got caught by that sprinkler."

"Good thinking," said Al.

And off we all ran.

Mrs. Fisher was
in her garden,
watering her
petunias, when
we got there.

"Let me get right to the point," I said. "Mrs. Fisher, has a fat cat come by here recently?"

"Why, I thought I saw a cat that was wet," she said. "But I'm sure my eyes were just playing tricks."

"Why do you say that?" I asked.

"Well, it seems so silly to say, but this wet, fat cat had a blue bonnet on its head."

"Then I wasn't seeing things," she said.
"Goodness, I thought I was just getting
old."

"Do you remember where the cat went?"
I asked.

Why, yes. It went over toward Mr. Snipeman's yard.

"SNIPEMONSTER'S YARD!" we all yelled.

"Oh no!"

Chapter 3

Snipemonster lived alone in a big, dark house. His real name was Mr. Snipeman, but we called him Snipemonster. All the children were scared of him. We didn't know if he was mean or just plain creepy because nobody ever talked to him. Most kids on the block had never even seen him.

As we started to leave, I noticed something on the ground.

There were paw prints
in the mud. They were
going out of
Mrs. Fisher's yard.
"I'll bet
they're Wendall's," I said.
"Let's follow them."

Step by step we followed the paw prints.

Just as Mrs. Fisher had said, they led to Snipemonster's lawn. But the strange thing was, the paw prints suddenly stopped.

Look, they've disappeared!

"It's like magic," said Billy.

"In all the years I have been a detective,"
I said, "I have never met a cat who could
do magic."

Wendall had to have gone somewhere.
Cats don't just vanish into air.

"Maybe he climbed up a tree," said Al.

"I don't see any tree," I said.

"Or maybe he fell in a hole and is trying to dig himself out," suggested Billy.

"There is no hole," I said.

"I bet a couple of cat burglars picked him up and are holding him for ransom," said Annie.

"Or maybe aliens came to Earth and beamed Wendall up to their spaceship," said Al.

SNIPEMONSTER!

Chapter 4

"Yeah, but come look at the ground and see what I found," I said.

"Where Wendall's prints disappear, another set of prints begin. And these are HUMAN footprints. The only way that Wendall could have disappeared would be if someone picked him up," I said.

41

"Solving the case was easy," I said. "Getting Wendall back from Snipemonster is going to be the tricky part."

Annie started to cry.

We needed a plan. So I came up with one: "Maybe if we snuck up to the porch, we could find a way into the house, grab Wendall and escape without Snipemonster even knowing."

"Do you want the cat back or not?" I asked. Annie and Al nodded. "That's what I thought. Now let's go."

I wasn't too happy about this whole idea myself, but there was no time to lose. I had a job to do.

We moved forward.

Inch by inch.

Step by step.

Slowly.

Carefully.

Finally we made it all the way to
Snipemonster's front porch.

Just then, a board creaked.

We held our breath and waited.

Quietly, we heard the lock unlock.

Suddenly,

the knob twisted.

And the door began to open.

What a surprise!
There stood a little
old man. He looked
like a cartoon
character, but I was
still suspicious.

"We're looking for Wendall," I said. "Al and Annie's fat cat."

Wendall?

Yes, Wendall. Is he here?

"You are very clever to have figured out to come here," he said. "As a matter of fact, I do have your cat."

"This Wendall came by the other day all wet and tangled up in the strings of a bonnet. I didn't know whom it belonged to. So I brought the cat into the house. And then that critter went and hid in the basement!"

Wendall in Snipemonster's basement! This was getting worse all the time.

"Can you give him back now?" I asked.

"I'd like to, but Wendall isn't ready to leave yet. There is a little family business to take care of first."

I knew it!
He's killed him!

Snipemonster
started to laugh.

"What's so funny?" we asked.

Down,

down,

down

into the dank, musty basement,
Snipemonster led us. A big box was on
the floor in a dark corner.

"You can look at your cat, but Wendall
won't be able to leave for a while."

"Why not?"

Snipemonster was cackling so hard
now that he had to hold on to his side.

"Look in the box," he said, when he'd
caught his breath.

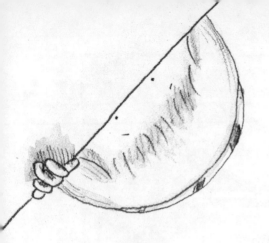

We bent down and peeked
inside the box.

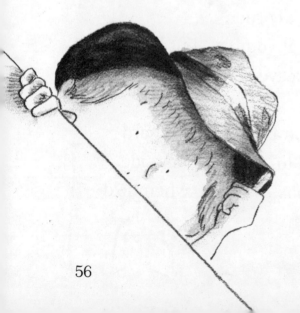

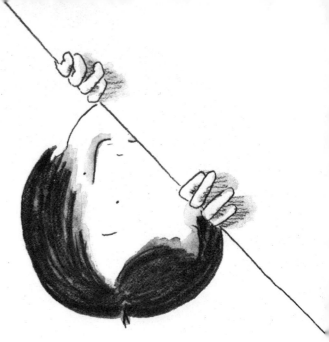

Being a detective,
I thought I had seen it all.
But not this!

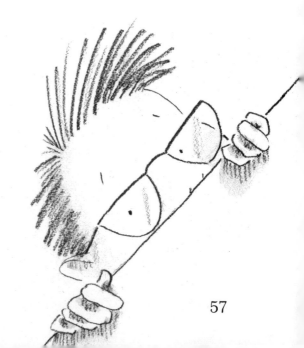

"WENDALL?!"

And that is where this caper ends. I
should add that Al and Annie gave
Snipemonster, er, I mean, Mr. Snipeman
one of the kittens—a boy. He named him
Wendall. We visit the two of them all the
time.

For helping to solve the case, Al said
I could have a kitten, too. But I said that I
would just rather name them. I called
them Mo, Jo and Flo.

Because,

the only thing

I like as much as solving

crimes is making

rhymes.